Celebraciones / Celebrations

¡Feliz día del padre!

Happy Father's Day!

Ada Kinney

traducido por / translated by

Fatima Rateb

PowerKiDS press.

New York

Published in 2017 by The Rosen Publishing Group, Inc.
29 East 21st Street, New York, NY 10010

First Edition

Translator: Fatima Rateb
Editorial Director, Spanish: Nathalie Beullens-Maoui
Editor, English: Melissa Raé Shofner
Book Design: Michael Flynn
Illustrator: Continuum Content Solutions

Cataloging-in-Publication Data

Names: Kinney, Ada, author.
Title: Happy Father's Day! = ¡Feliz día del padre! / Ada Kinney.
Description: New York : PowerKids Press, [2017] | Series: Celebrations = Celebraciones |
   Includes index.
Identifiers: ISBN 9781499428438 (library bound)
Subjects: LCSH: Father's Day–Juvenile literature.
Classification: LCC HQ756.5 .K56 2017 | DDC 394.263–dc23

Manufactured in the United States of America

CPSIA Compliance Information: Batch #BW17PK: For Further Information contact Rosen Publishing, New York, New York at 1-800-237-9932

Contenido

Contents

¡Hoy es el Día del Padre!

Today is Father's Day!

4

Bilingual Books Collection

California Immigrant Alliance Project

Funded by
The California State Library

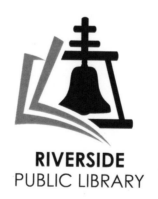

RIVERSIDE
PUBLIC LIBRARY

Voy a pasar el día con mi papá.

I will spend the day with my dad.

Preparamos el desayuno juntos.

We make breakfast together.

Mi papá hace huevos. Yo hago tostadas.

My dad makes eggs. I make toast.

A mi papá le gusta correr.

Corremos a menudo juntos.

My dad likes to jog. We often jog together.

¡Papá, ve más despacio!

Slow down, Dad!

9

Luego, vamos a un juego de béisbol.

Later, we go to a baseball game.

Aplaudimos y animamos al equipo.

We clap and cheer.

¡Nuestro equipo gana el juego!

Our team wins the game!

Papá, ¡choca esos cinco!

I give my dad a high five.

Mi papá y yo nos compramos
unas gorras iguales.

My dad and I buy matching hats.

Es hora de comer pizza.

Then it's time to eat pizza.

15

Contamos chistes de regreso a casa.

We tell jokes on the drive home.

¡Mi papá es muy gracioso!

My dad is very funny!

Mi papá me lee un libro
antes de irme a dormir.
Es sobre gatitos. Él imita
voces chistosas.

My dad reads me a book
before bed. It's about
kittens. He uses silly voices.

Me da sueño cuando lee.

I get sleepy when he reads.

Después del cuento, le
doy a mi papá una tarjeta.

After the story, I give
my dad a card.

Hice un dibujo de nosotros dos.

I drew a picture of us.

22

Mi papá está muy contento. ¡Te quiero, papá!

My dad is very happy. I love you, Dad!

Palabras que debes aprender
Words to Know

(el) desayuno
breakfast

(la) tarjeta
card

correr
jog

Índice / Index

24